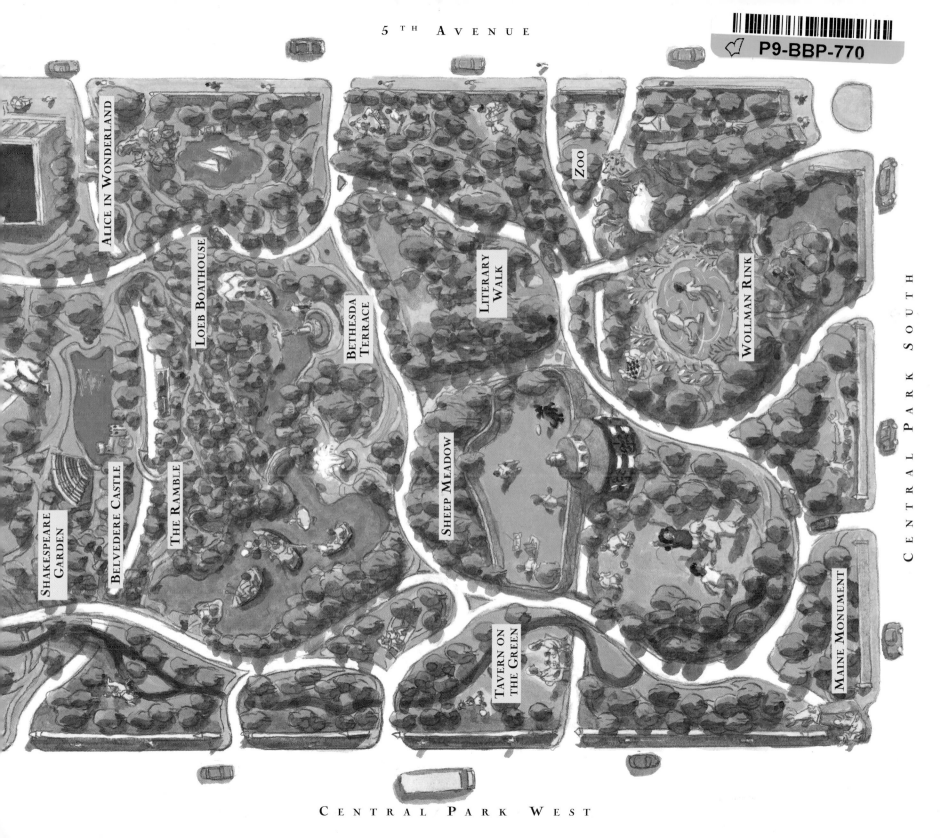

For Henry —L.G.

For Kim, with a certain path across the park in mind,
and where it led —B.R.

Central Park Serenade Text © 2002 by Laura Godwin Illustrations copyright © 2002 by Barrett V. Root Manufactured in China.
All rights reserved. www.harperchildrens.com Library of Congress Cataloging-in-Publication Data Godwin, Laura.   Central Park
serenade / by Laura Godwin ; pictures by Barry Root.   p.   cm.   "Joanna Cotler books."   Summary: Illustrations and
rhyming text celebrate the sights and sounds of New York's Central Park in summer.   ISBN 0-06-025891-8. — ISBN 0-06-025892-
6 (lib. bdg.)   [1. Central Park (New York, N.Y.)–Fiction. 2. Stories in rhyme.] I. Root, Barry, ill. II. Title.
PZ8.3.B846Cg 2002 99-50279 [E]—dc21 CIP Typography by Alicia Mikles   4 5 6 7 8 9 10 ❖ First Edition

CENTRAL PARK
SERENADE

By LAURA GODWIN

Pictures by
BARRY ROOT

JOANNA COTLER BOOKS
An Imprint of HarperCollins*Publishers*

Beep, beep, beep,
A taxi calls.
But the traffic creeps and the traffic crawls.

Honk, honk, honk.
A bus drives by.
A startled baby starts to cry.

And the pigeons coo
And the big dogs bark
And the noises echo through the park.

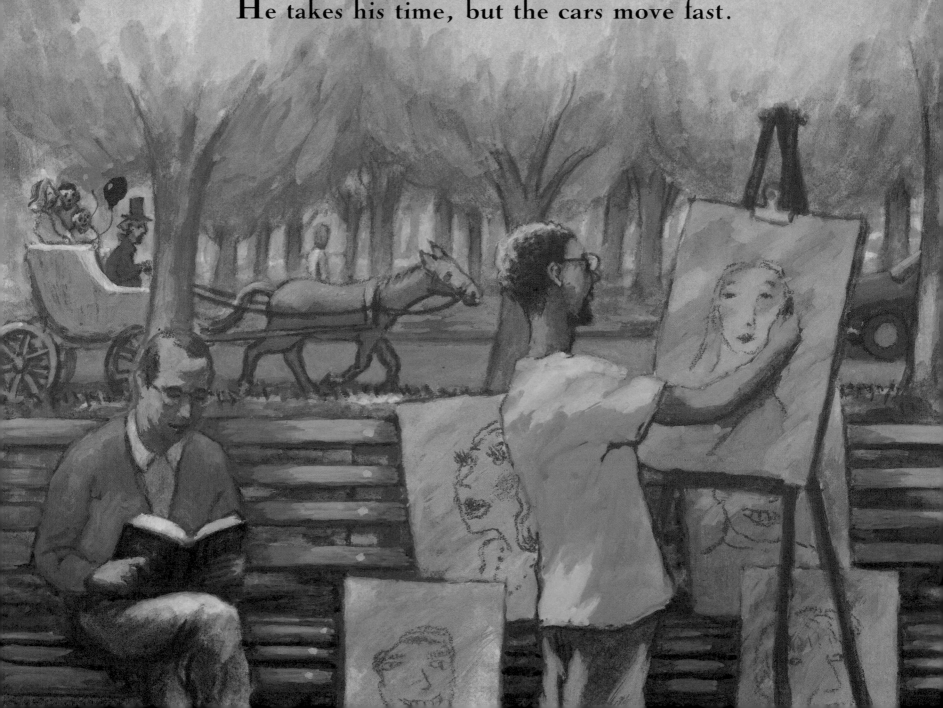

Clip clop, clip clop.

A horse trots past.

He takes his time, but the cars move fast.

A skater skates, and her wheels spin round.
A bike's brakes squeal, and you hear the sound.

And the pigeons coo
And the big dogs bark
And the noises echo through the park.

Boom, boom, boom,
A drummer plays
As the sun sends down its summer rays

A breeze blows by the biker's face
While a jogger seems to run in place.

And the pigeons coo
And the big dogs bark
And the noises echo through the park.

Striike one! Striike two! An umpire's call.
Craaack! Whoosh! retorts the ball.
Pat pat pat go the players' feet.
Pant pant pant in the summer heat.

And the pigeons coo
And the big dogs bark
And the noises echo through the park.

Ice-cold! Ice cream! Lemonade!
Sticky cone, tall-tree shade.

Water spraying, children walk.
Babies playing, nannies talk.

And the pigeons coo
And the big dogs bark
And the noises echo through the park.

Parents calling, "Time for dinner!"
Crowds dispersing, growing thinner.
Shadows merge, becoming one.
Then the summer day is done.

And the pigeons coo
And the dogs still bark
But sleep has come to Central Park.

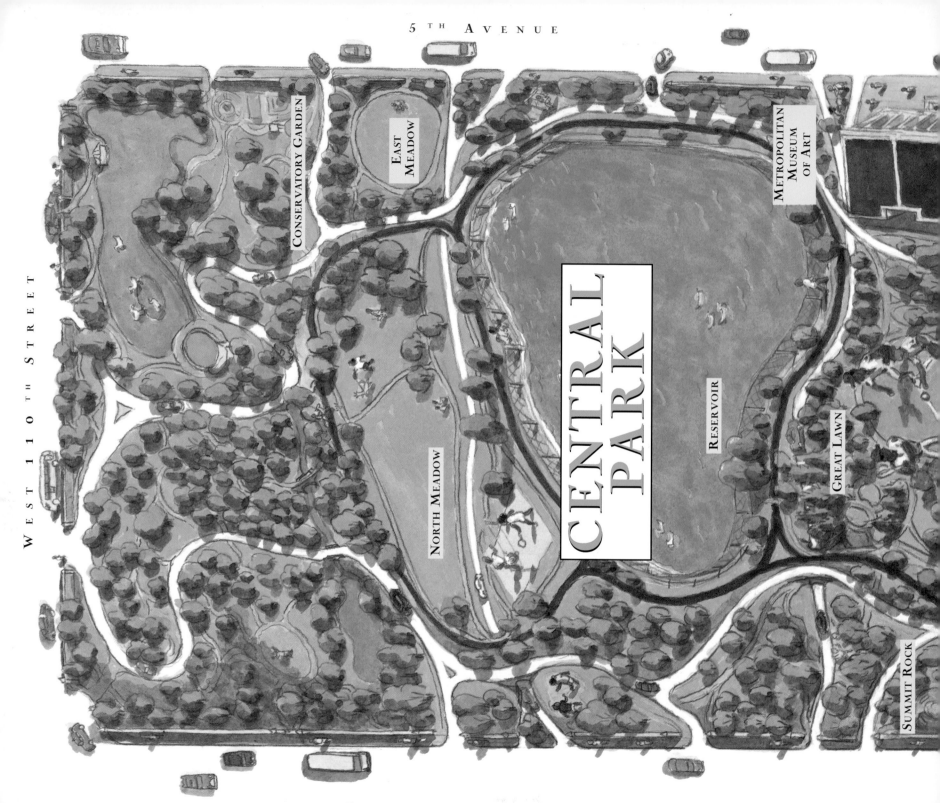

5TH AVENUE

WEST 110TH STREET

CONSERVATORY GARDEN

EAST MEADOW

METROPOLITAN MUSEUM OF ART

CENTRAL PARK

RESERVOIR

NORTH MEADOW

GREAT LAWN

SUMMIT ROCK

CENTRAL PARK WEST